This Book
Belongs To:

_____

_____

GW00728135

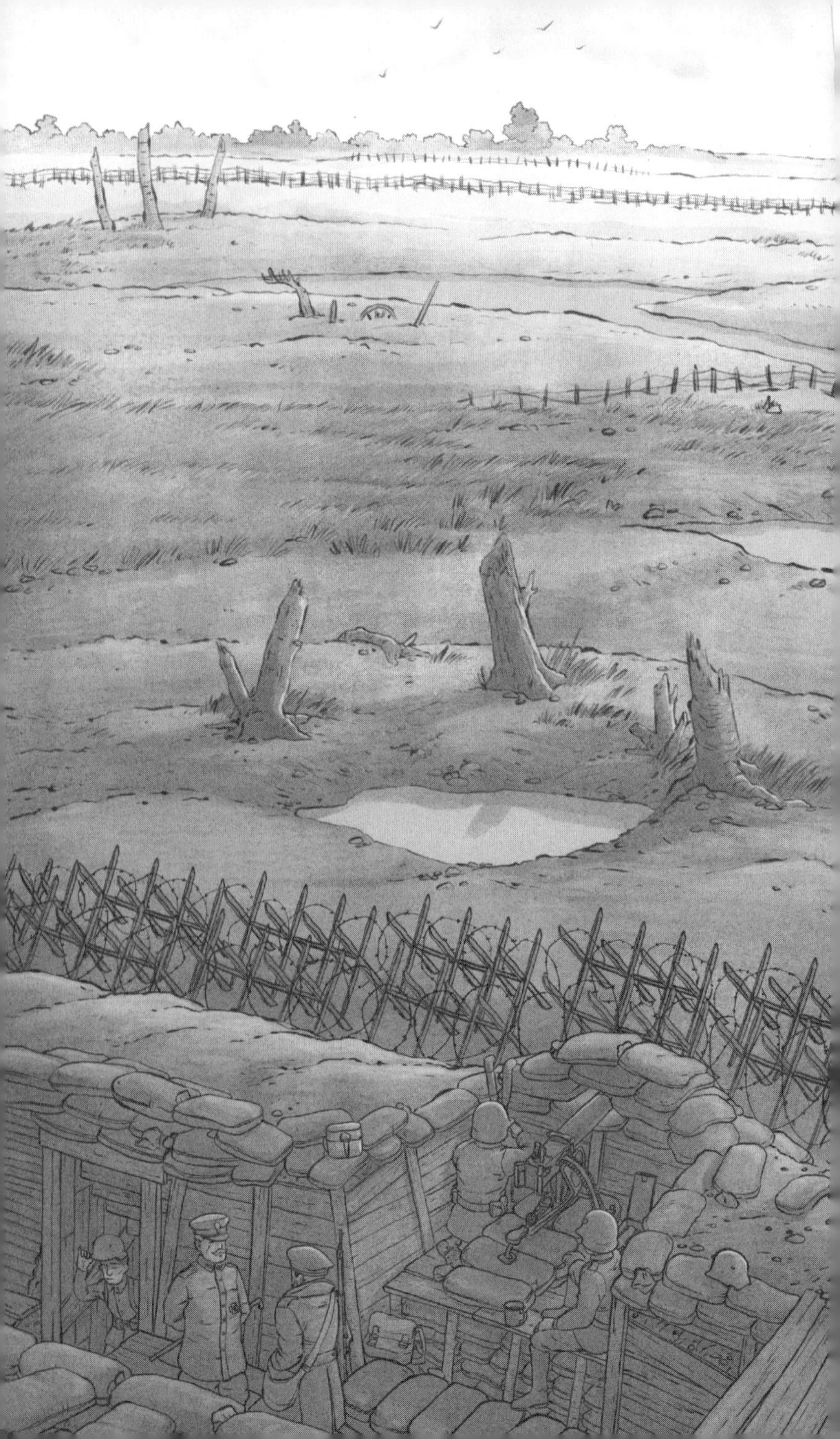

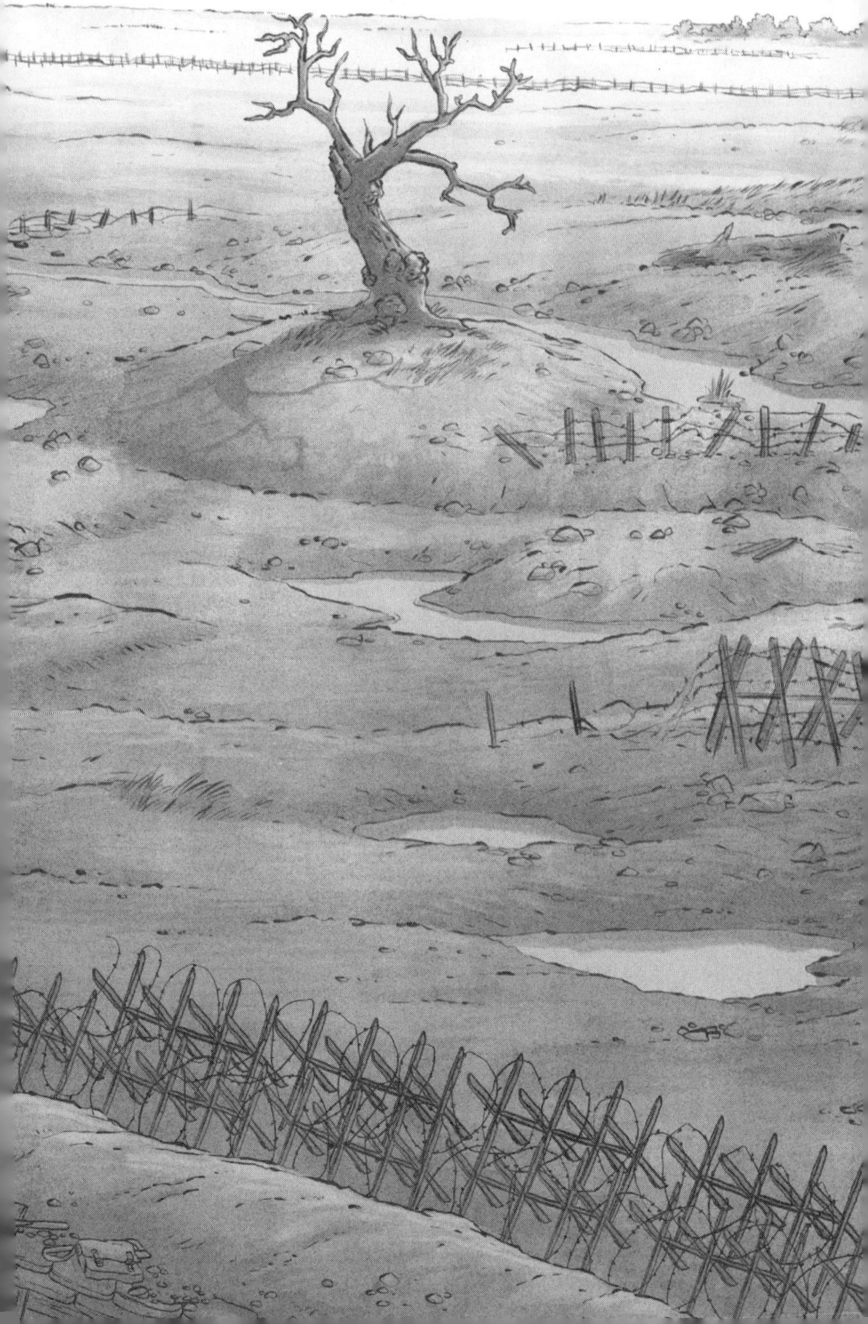

First published 2021 © Twinkl Ltd of Wards Exchange,
197 Ecclesall Road, Sheffield S11 8HW

ISBN: 978-1-914331-32-9

Copyright © Twinkl Ltd. 2021

All rights reserved. No part of this book may be reproduced in any form or by any
means, electronic or mechanical, including photocopying, recording or by any
information and retrieval system, without permission in writing from Twinkl Ltd.

This is a work of fiction. Names, characters, businesses, places, events and incidents
are either the products of the author's imagination or used in a fictitious manner. Any
resemblance to actual persons, living or dead, or actual events is purely coincidental.

We're passionate about giving our children a sustainable future, which is why this book
is made from Forest Stewardship Council® certified paper. Learn how our Twinkl Green
policy gives the planet a helping hand at www.twinkl.com/twinkl-green.

Printed in the United Kingdom.

10 9 8 7 6 5 4 3 2 1

A catalogue record for this book is available from the British Library.

Twinkl is a registered trademark of Twinkl Ltd.

A TWINKL ORIGINAL

The *Birds* of Flanders Fields

Twinkl Educational Publishing

Contents

No Man's Land

1916

A spindly tree stands in a carpet of mud. Really, it is the remains of what was once a tree. It is alive, barely. There are no leaves and no colour. Brittle, broken branches fork towards the sky.

Nothing much grows here any more. Snapped and splintered wood is strangled by snatches of razor-sharp wire.

A small, grey-headed bird flies unsteadily, inches above the uneven ground. He heaves himself upwards and lands on one of the jagged branches of the tree.

A high-pitched scream rings through the air, like a wounded gull. It is followed by the shattering *boom* of an explosion nearby.

Another bird flaps ungracefully from the opposite direction, weaves through the smoky haze and lands on the same low branch as the first.

"Hey!" she chirrups.

"Um. Hello."

Half a furlong to one side lie tangled rolls of the razor-sharp wire. Not so long ago, the wire was held up by wooden stumps. Now, the loops of wire are swallowing the stumps, dragging them down.

Half a furlong to the other side are matching rolls of wire and stumps. These stand a little taller. Both are equally impenetrable barriers for any land creatures. No more than the width of a standard field separates the two sides, as the crow flies.

There are other trees in the land in-between – remains of what were once trees. They tilt and lean like wonky scarecrows in a field – but this field has no crops. It is muddied and damaged and scarred.

"I'm Lucky" says the grey-headed bird nervously.

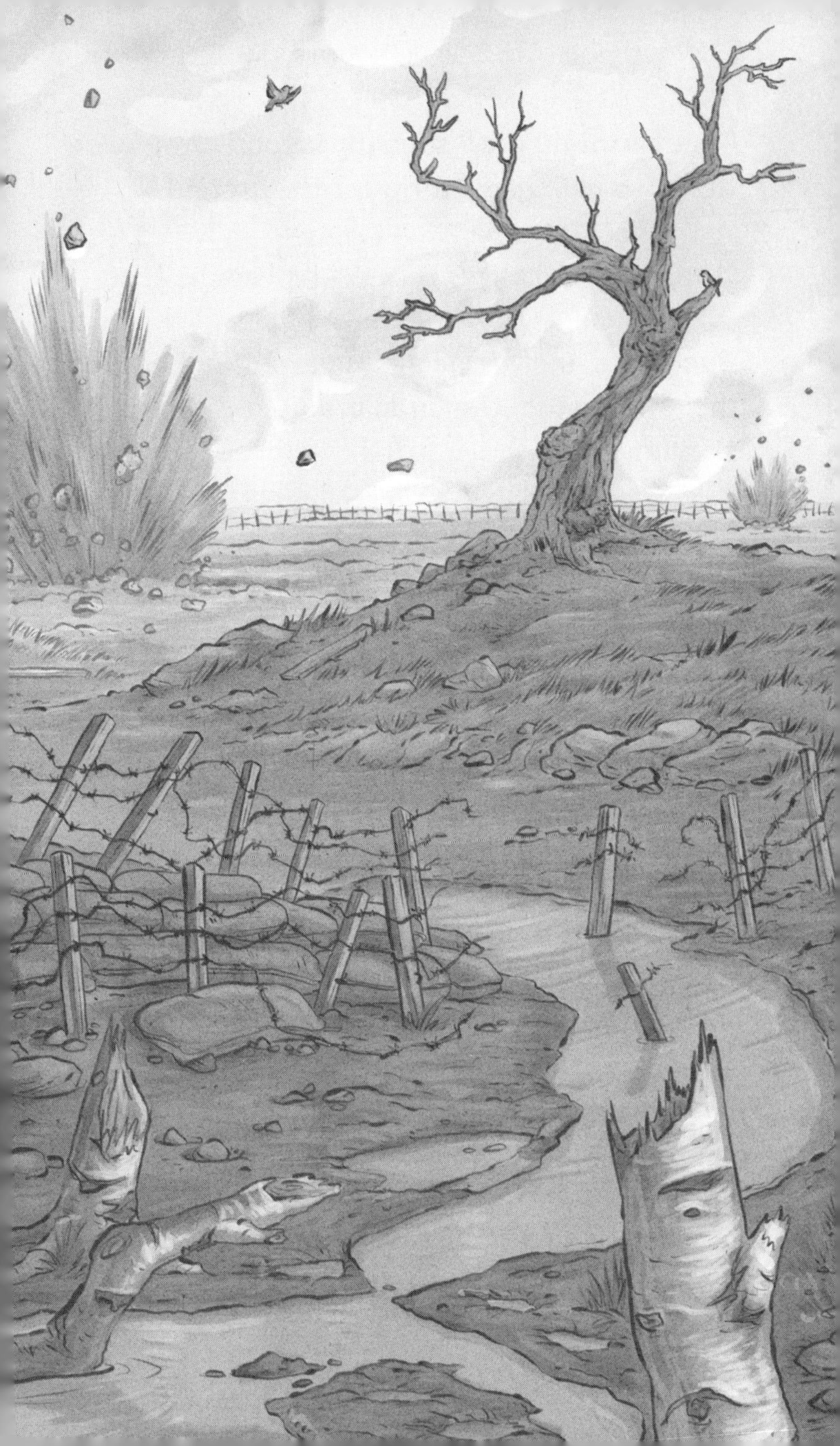

"You certainly are," says the second. "You were flying so low, you nearly hit the ground."

"Um. No, I'm called 'Lucky'," replies the first.

Bang goes another deafening explosion. Though they are young, the birds are used to it and do not flinch.

A burning smell seeps through the air. It's a smell that comes and goes often, mixing with a rotting stench from the ground. Lucky has heard the elder birds chittering about the fresh scents of spring from years ago. He dreams of fresh flower smells.

"Are you one of the finches?" asks the second bird.

"Yes, a chaffinch," says Lucky. "Are you a kind of sparrow?"

"Yes. I'm Buffy. I'm a tree sparrow. Mother says I'm not a fledgling any more. I can fly."

"I can fly, too. I'm just not very good at it yet."

Buffy looks hard at him. "Wait. You're not *the* lucky chaffinch, are you? Lucky Half-Wing?" she asks.

"That's me! How do you know?" says Lucky in surprise.

"Everyone has heard of you hatching. You survived when your nest was blown out of the tree. You're special!"

"That's what Pa says. But not so special – this wing only half opens." He demonstrates by stretching out his wings as far as they will go. The right one reaches about half as far as the left.

The tree shakes as the ground rumbles. Lucky twitches and turns his head with short, sharp movements. Both birds keep all their surroundings in sight, always. It's basic bird survival. It's more important here than anywhere.

"Where was your nest?" asks Lucky.

"Over there, to the east – on the side of one of

the huge firing machines," says Buffy. "It makes such loud bangs. When we were hatchlings, I was closest to the bangs."

"Wow! Sounds like you were lucky to survive, too."

"No one calls *me* 'lucky'. I can't hear properly on this side." She twitches her head to the left.

The pair of birds perch in the tree. They chitter and cheep. The bangs and whistles and explosions come in waves. Sometimes, there is movement and noise from the humans in their ditches at each side. Sometimes, the figures lie still, staring silently across the space between.

"I haven't been to the east yet. I'm not allowed. What's it like?" asks Lucky.

"Well, there is the Land of No Man's, where we are. Then, there is sharp wire. Next, there are ditches where the humans shuffle around in the ground. There is more land after that but I don't know it well," Buffy explains.

"That's the same as on the west!" Lucky flicks

his head and points his beak towards his home.

"Really?"

"Yep!" He nods animatedly. "At the edge of the Land of No Man's on this side is also sharp wire. Then, human ditches. Then, more land."

Buffy gives a chirp and looks thoughtfully to Lucky's side in the west.

More birds are all around. They chitter to each other. A baby robin comes and goes. He flies away to seek food, then returns. Fresh out of his nest, he is extra cautious. He does not dare to land or hover anywhere for long.

A pair of blackbirds hop along the bare earth in the Land of No Man's. They are flitting between nest and ground. In nearby trees, there are skylarks and swallows, warblers and whitethroats.

"Do you think everywhere is like this?" Buffy asks.

"Like what?"

"The bangs. The danger. The humans in their ditches. The sharp wire. The firing machines attacking the land."

"I don't think so," says Lucky. "Ma says it's only been like this here for a summer and a half. Some faraway places are peaceful. Not even any humans. There are meadows and woodlands, green fields and sweet flowers. She says the sharp wire wasn't here until the humans came."

"Why must we live here, then, if it is full of danger?"

"Pa says we were here first. It's home – but in the winter, we'll do the Big Journey."

"I can't wait to see the faraway places," says Buffy. "I hope that when we come back, it is more peaceful here."

*

Day after day, the two birds are back on the same branch. They chirrup and chirp about the day's events. Their new feathers come in and they become juveniles. It is their first summer. This land is the only land they've ever known, but they dream of the faraway places talked about by the elder birds.

The days grow longer. The sun shines brighter. In the distance, wildflowers start to appear – but not in the Land of No Man's. Here, the land is nothing but brown. It is trampled and torn up. The morning sun is reflected in craters pooled with murky water. Some craters are the size of a nest; others are as wide as a whole bush. More bangs and whistles blight the air: crashing, booming, thudding.

As the sun sets and rises again, the sky grows busier with birds. Hatchlings have fledged. Juveniles are more confident flyers. The last

9

migrants have returned from their Big Journeys of last winter. All the other birds know of Lucky and Buffy: one who can't fly straight and one who can't hear well. They perch together in the Spindly Tree. They fly together to Lucky's side of the Land of No Man's. They fly together to Buffy's side. They do not settle anywhere. They prefer it in the Spindly Tree where they can look from one side to the other.

All the other birds know of them. Not all of them approve.

"You two should be more careful," a menacing kestrel warns them. He has hunched shoulders

and cutting eyes. He sits defiantly on a piece of metal casing, which juts out from the side of a crater at the base of the Spindly Tree. The curved metal protrudes from the mud where it is lodged. It is one of many that lie half buried.

Lucky twitches his head anxiously. Buffy turns and focuses an eye on the kestrel.

"Why is a chaffinch to be found with a tree sparrow?" the kestrel asks suspiciously. "Why are you not with your own flocks?"

"We're friends, that's all," replies Buffy. Lucky shuffles his small, clawed feet along the ground. He feels his wing ache. It always aches when he's anxious.

"You are innocent juveniles," the kestrel scoffs. "I've seen you flying over both sides. That is not how it works. There is great danger in the land between. You should pick a side and stay there."

The kestrel spreads his sizeable wings and launches from his metal resting place. He soars away, occasionally mirrored in the brown pools as he passes above them. Then, he is absorbed into the distance. His grim warning hangs in the air after he is gone.

Lucky glances at Buffy and then tilts his head and looks around. Short, sharp jerks of his stout, little neck accompany each thought that enters his mind. His tail twitches. His wing throbs. He looks back at Buffy again.

"Do we have to pick a side?" Lucky asks. He glances across the Land of No Man's from one side to the other. Of course, he already understands that there is danger. There is always danger for birds. Humans rarely enter the Land of No Man's, however. That is one good thing. That is how it was named.

"We could ask the Elders," offers Buffy, helpfully.

"Yes! Good idea!" replies the lucky chaffinch. They both launch from the ground and leave the Spindly Tree behind.

*

The Elders have all lived for more than three summers. Some of them have flown the Big

Journey even more times than that. A very small few have lived for ten or more summers and winters.

The birds come from all flocks. They congregate together every fourth sunset. Their dusk meeting place is marked by three branchless trunks which rise from the mud.

Lucky and Buffy circle overhead. The ground below is scattered with stones and debris, and other birds fly in and out. No one stays for long. That is normal for birds. Here, time on the ground is even more limited. Time with the Elders is precious and rare.

A cuckoo with layers of grey plumage sits proudly atop one of the tree stumps. A wise nightingale keeps her watchful eyes on the surroundings, hopping, twisting and scanning. An ageing yellowhammer and a pair of old blackbirds are also present.

One of the blackbirds bounds lightly along the ground. He is a master of scavenging, and there are always insects to be found in the Land of No Man's. Scurrying beetles, woodlice and earwigs love this ground because of the rotting. Earthworms try to burrow and hide but the blackbirds know just how to coax them from their hidden nooks.

Not all of the Elders are present; however, there are always some to consult. Lucky and Buffy fly down to the ground to join the assembled birds. One of the blackbirds is black, like the name; the other is brown.

Lucky zig-zags down towards the ground and lands askew. Soil flicks up and he shakes it off. The cuckoo gives a look of disapproval.

Buffy touches down to his right. Her claws barely touch the ground before she gives a twist, a spin and a quick study of all sides. Settling, she dances lightly from side to side. The blackbirds are searching for worms. They don't look pleased at the interruption.

"What brings you here?" asks the yellowhammer from the sidelines, eyeing them suspiciously. As his name suggests, he is streaked with yellow. He is small but stocky. Though well preened, his feathers are aged and timeworn. Buffy recognises him from the woodland on the east side, where the yellowhammer flock nests.

"Excuse us. We have a question." She hesitates but there is no reply, so she goes on. "Do you all pick a side to stay on? Or do you fly everywhere?"

"A side?" the cuckoo replies. "What good is a side? There are humans on both sides. We fly where there is food. We feed. We fly to our nests. That is all that matters."

"What about when danger comes?" Lucky presses.

"There is always danger, young one," says the brown blackbird. "Where there are humans, there is danger. Be alert. You must always be alert!" She bounces along the ground as she chirps. Occasionally, she pecks at the compacted earth.

Suddenly, an explosion shatters the surrounding stillness. It is not close but is within view.

Instinctively, all the Elders scatter to the skies.

"Fly quick, fly quick," calls the cuckoo. Yet, he is the slowest to lift off and he appears to flap more laboriously than the others.

In the air, Lucky glances at Buffy. He wonders whether it will be a short danger – over with quickly – or one where they must retreat to the more distant trees.

The answer comes with the swifts. The entire flock swoops through the Land of No Man's. Their screaming call accompanies the moaning and whistling of the firing machines. This is a sign that there could be grave danger on its way.

Humans bellow from the ditch on one side. Lucky and Buffy are still airborne together, wings beating frantically. Piercing shrieks fill the air. Each shriek is followed by bellows and booms. Another, then another. Closer. The birds peel away from where the sound is loudest. The swifts turn and loop, then dive through the air again. Everyone senses that they are herding. It means that it is time to flee.

The Spindly Tree is not safe right now. Buffy signals to Lucky that they should fly west. The bangs are occurring in the east right now. Lucky opens his left wing and then forces his right one as far as it will go. He feels it ache more and winces. They touch down briefly on a tree on the western side.

"Um. Is this how we pick a side?" asks Lucky.

"We are picking this side right now," the young tree sparrow replies, "only because it is the safe side to pick today. Tomorrow might be different. Just pick the side that is safe. You heard what the blackbird said: be alert."

The pair sit for a while and watch as the twilight fades away. The Land of No Man's is gradually filling with smoke. Soil is thrown up in angry blasts. Great force pounds the ground. New craters are slashed into the earth.

This is what it is like: the quiet, then the barrage.

"Why does it happen?" Lucky asks. "Why do they tear up the earth?"

"Mother says the humans brought the danger upon the Land of No Man's. No one knows why."

"Perhaps we can find out," Lucky suggests. "Perhaps we can help to stop it."

"Not right now." The reply comes from the arrival of Lucky's father. His chaffinch markings are similar to Lucky's. They each have a long, brown tail with white edging. Lucky has very small patches of olive green, but Pa has much broader ones. He lands beside Lucky momentarily and looks solemnly at his offspring. "We must flee. Farther than usual. Say farewell. We will return."

Lucky looks at Buffy. He snaps his head to the left and the right and up and down. He sees the dangers and knows Pa is right. There is a whistling overhead, then the ground is ripped apart, only a few tree lengths away. The noise is painful. Clouds of dust mix with the dark, smoky air. The scent of the earth melds with a burning odour. It is both unpleasant and unsafe for flying.

Through the mist, Buffy sees her mother and siblings and cousins. Lucky signals goodbye to

Buffy and takes flight with Pa. Buffy mingles with her flock and they fly farther beyond the west side. They leave behind field after field. Lucky and Pa have joined the chaffinch flock. They, too, head along the west side but farther away from Buffy and the tree sparrows. Larks swoop and dive to lead the way. Pa says that they must venture past the human ditches this time – farther than Lucky has been before.

As they fly, Lucky is shocked at how many ditches he sees scarring the dark ground. Humans are scurrying along many of them. They, too, look panicked.

"There are rows and rows," he chirps into the air. No one is close enough to listen or to hear. His chirps are carried away by the breeze, dwarfed by the bangs and booms behind them. "What are the humans doing?"

Swifts dart and dive in the sky up ahead. Lucky sees the warblers and many other finches. They have not come so far that the bangs can't still be heard, but they are far enough away to feel safer. Many birds descend onto a row of poplar trees to hunker away until dawn reveals the vibrant colours of the place they have reached.

Lucky sees flowers. On one side of the poplars, there is a field of yellow buttercups and dandelions. Near a hedgerow on the far side, a scattering of bright red poppies grow. On the other side of the hedge, there is another field of green. It is lined with rows and rows of peculiar wooden crosses. They look like they are growing from the ground, too.

A stone building stands beyond the other side of the poplars. It is empty apart from a family of sand martins who are zipping in and out. Lucky wonders if Buffy is somewhere safe.

*

Quiet eventually comes after several more sunsets of relentless danger. A line of tree sparrows gather on a communication telegraph wire. Buffy is among them. They are not in the Land of No Man's. They are on the west side of a row of human ditches. Buffy leaves the flock and swoops over the humans' heads towards the Spindly Tree.

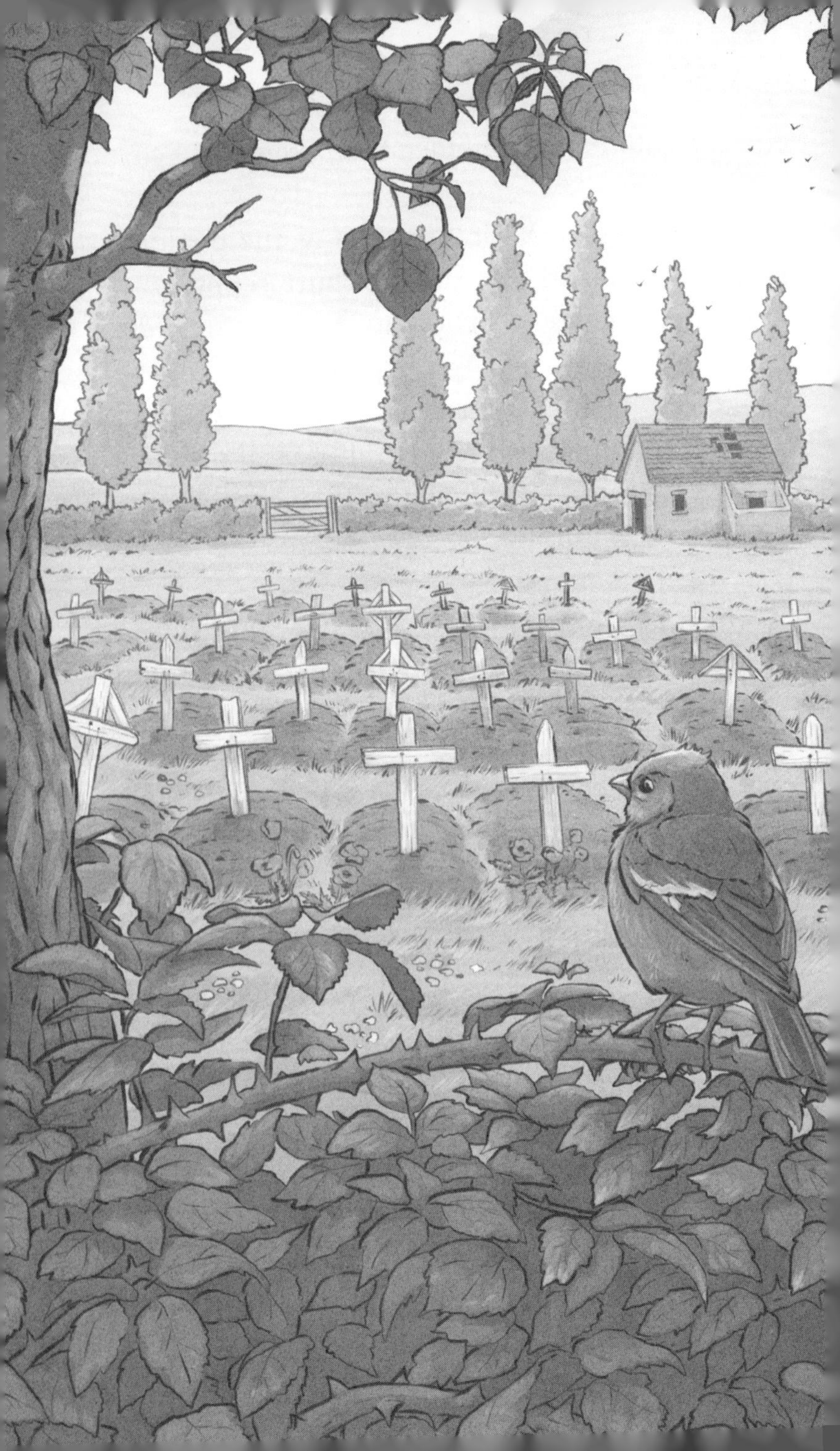

Farther along the Land of No Man's, flocks mingle together. The birds are returning along with the quiet. Warblers, blackcaps and chaffinches perch on branches. Lucky is with the finch flock. His head twitches and turns quicker than the others. He stays aware of everything and everyone. Pa said that it was safe to return. They are still on the edge of the land considered 'home'. It is a wary return.

Lucky's limp wing means he is not as fast a flyer as his siblings or cousins. He has kept up with them as best he could. However, his sight makes up for his lack of speed. He checks all angles, listens, checks again. He can see across the Land of No Man's.

He swoops to the Spindly Tree and sees Buffy. His heart soars. Buffy dances her claws on the branch, excitedly.

"You are safe!" says Buffy.

"You are, too!" replies Lucky.

Although other birds visit it, it feels like *their* Spindly Tree, now. Its ragged branches make familiar lines against the sky. They are glad to be back here. They are even more glad to be back together.

"I thought the danger might never end this time," Buffy continues. "We flew to the fields but could still hear the bangs going on and on."

"So did we. Not everywhere looks just like here," says Lucky. "Away from the Land of No Man's, there are prettier places. There are flowers! Yellows and reds and greens."

"Yes, I saw them, too! Mother was right," says Buffy sadly. "The danger is here because of the humans."

"Just like Ma and Pa said," agrees Lucky.

They rest on the branch of the Spindly Tree. The sunrises and sunsets bring more quiet and then, more danger. Not so much danger to flee this time. Then, more quiet again. No one knows when the danger will restart – or when it will stop – until it happens.

News has filtered through the flocks. There

are rumours that the Land of No Man's was invaded by humans while they were away. Lucky ponders, not for the first time, over their purpose in attacking the land that lies between the ditches.

Some birds didn't follow the herding of the swifts. Some stayed. Now, one of the whitethroats is missing and some think that it has not survived the danger. Lucky has heard of this before: a bird goes away and never returns. He hopes this never happens to Buffy. Or to Ma and Pa.

It is not long before summer bleeds into autumn. The time for the Big Journey arrives. Lucky and Buffy must go separately with their flocks.

"We must all have hope that the dangers will be gone when we return," Buffy says as they leave.

"I hope so," Lucky agrees. "If not, I think we must find out why it happens."

"Fly safely," Buffy instructs him.

"Listen carefully," Lucky says in return.

Return to Flanders Fields

1917

Lucky sits in the Spindly Tree. It is weathered and beaten. The tree has stood without him for a whole winter. There appear to be fewer trees here now than when he followed Pa away for the Big Journey. Thankfully, the Spindly Tree remains, casting its scrawny shadow on the Land of No Man's. Lucky has missed its long limbs. Not as much as he has missed Buffy, though. There is, so far, no sign of her returning. He shakes out his feathers and waits.

Most birds leave for the Big Journey each winter. Some go farther than others. Sometimes, it is a search for warmer weather. Those who return must find new nesting spots. The humans have not left, however. A chitter of rumours is passed through the flocks about their presence. The nesting spots are more dangerous than ever.

Lucky wishes that his home had safer nesting spots. He has been back for days. There are already new nests in treacherous locations: inside an empty metal shell on the ground; on the giant firing machines. He thinks back to his own time as a nestling and the nest that was blown out of the tree. The wing that still aches. He thinks of Buffy's nest, next to the big firing machine. Those bangs which affected her hearing. He thinks of Buffy.

The bangs have not gone away. Everything here is the same: danger, noise, desolation.

"Buffy!" he suddenly cries.

His best friend emerges from the sky. More gracefully than before, she lands next to him on their branch, in their tree. Her flying is so much more refined, now.

"You're here," she chirrups merrily.

"I didn't think you were coming back." Lucky chirps his relief.

For many sunrises and many sunsets, the pair

exchange stories of their Big Journeys. Buffy and her mother travelled farther. Both tell tales of the sights they saw. Both found peaceful skies and prettier places.

"I had so hoped it would be peaceful again here when we returned," Buffy sighs.

"Nothing has changed," agrees Lucky.

"I think it may even be worse," suggests Buffy.

They look around, heads darting sharply from one direction to the next. The Land of No Man's looks even more brown than before. More churned-up earth, more craters, more hard-to-identify remains. It is a murky landscape, lacking life or colour. From their position in the Spindly Tree, Lucky can see the tangles of wire in the east and in the west. His eyesight is sharper than ever. He longs for his home to have flashes of cornflower blue, dandelion yellow and, most of all, poppy red.

Beyond the bundles of wire and broken wooden stumps, there are the ditches. Sandbags are piled into little walls at their sides. The fabric is worn and bleached by the sun.

"Maybe we could fly low over the human ditch," Buffy says. Her tail twitches. Her head tilts to glance at Lucky. "Maybe it's time to visit them and work out why they're here."

Lucky's tail twitches, too. His is an anxious twitch, rather than one of excitement. He casts his eye around for movement and ponders over Buffy's suggestion.

"You know what the Elders warn us. It's not safe near the humans. The humans have brought the danger," he mutters.

"Then, maybe we can find out how to help them make the danger go away again," Buffy insists.

"I don't know. It doesn't seem safe. Which humans and which ditches do we choose? Remember, the kestrel said that we should pick a side. The Elders said that where there are humans, there is danger."

"The Elders also said all that matters is food and flying. Let's visit both sides. Then, we can decide for ourselves."

Lucky doesn't know how to argue with Buffy. She is even braver than before. He wants the dangers to be over. Perhaps they can find out how to help that happen. Perhaps she is right.

*

The sun is at its highest in the sky. This is a time when there is usually quiet. Often, danger comes when the sun is low or has set. Shooting, firing, exploding.

Sometimes, danger lights up the sky as a warning. Sometimes, it sneaks through the darkness, then tears up the earth. Now, however, it is bright and sunny. Buffy declares that now is the perfect time. Lucky feels a twinge of pain in his wing.

The pair of birds – the chaffinch with a wonky wing and the tree sparrow who can't hear well – fly from their branch. They leave the Spindly Tree behind.

Lucky hovers over one of the human ditches to the west. A stump sticks up jauntily from the ground nearby. Maybe it is a tree stump or maybe it was a stump placed in the ground by humans. Cautiously, he lands on it. Buffy is braver. She lands right on a sun-bleached sandbag.

Life on the ground here is strange. The human ditches zig-zag and snake along below. Ditch after ditch is connected, like a maze. Some ditches have sheltered areas; some are open to the sun and the rain. Their walls are as high as the humans' heads. Some have wooden floors; some are swamped with mud. Lucky sees a rat running along the bottom, past human feet. The rodent is twice as big as Lucky. The chaffinch blinks his bulging eyes at the creature and twitches his wings.

Like magpies, the humans appear to collect many objects. They carry objects. They wear objects strapped around their bodies. The humans all have earth-coloured cloth coverings that make them look identical from head to foot. Their heads are also covered with hard, round metal. Almost all of them clutch those loud firing sticks.

"There are hundreds of humans," Lucky says.

"Maybe thousands," says Buffy.

"It's too dangerous," Lucky warns.

Some humans are standing or leaning. They do not, or cannot, keep themselves clean. Their feet are planted in mud. Some are sleeping. Others are slumped or sitting. None look happy. None look comfortable. Despite the rumours that it happens, the birds have never seen them leave these ditches for the land above. Not far from here, there are green fields. There are beautiful sights. Yet the humans choose to spend sunrise after sunrise in their ditch. This confuses Lucky.

One human looks up. He sees the birds.

Lucky freezes. The human stares straight at him while holding his firing stick across his front.

Buffy reacts quickly – she flies and is gone. From afar, she watches.

Lucky looks down at the human. Each of them gazes back at the other. Lucky's wing twitches. Then, the human smiles. His muddy face softens. There is a warmth to it.

Still wary, Lucky keeps his body still. His claws grip the wooden post. His head flicks from side to side. He is staying alert to any new danger.

Mainly, his attention is on the human, who moves slowly, reaching into a pouch. Lucky wants to launch and fly. At the same time, he does not dare. Still, his body remains frozen.

Slowly, purposefully, the human reaches out his arm. His hand is flat. He holds something. He motions with his upward palm. At the same time, he gives a tiny nod of his head. Lucky sees nothing else moving left or right. He focuses on the hand of the human. In it, there is food. The food is not berries or insects. A different food: tiny pieces, crumbs. He is offering it to Lucky.

Lucky does not know what to do or how to react. A human has never offered food before. Humans are supposed to be dangerous. He wonders if it is a trick or a trap. Yet the human's face shows kindness as he still looks up from out of the ditch. Again, he nods. Again, he motions with his hand. High above, Lucky thinks, stalls, wonders. Then, he decides.

In one fluid movement, the little chaffinch swoops. One wing holds strong; the other droops slightly. From the wooden stump, he glances onto the human's hand, pokes his beak clumsily

34

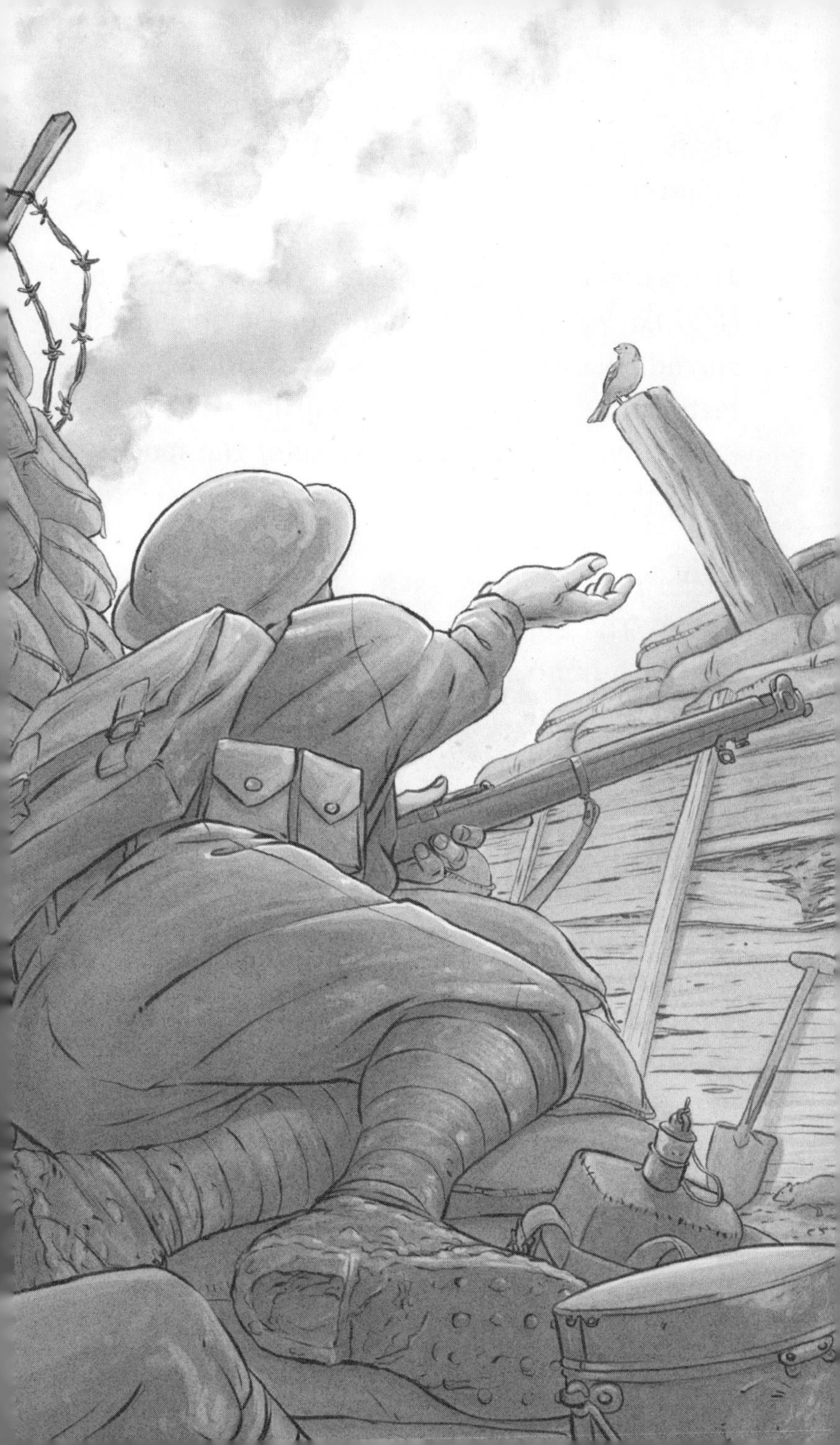

at the crumbs on offer, then flies swiftly away again to safety.

The crumbs are tasty. There is no trick, no trap. Now, Lucky feels like the brave one. More warmth spreads across the human's face. Yellowy-white teeth stand out against the grime of his skin. Lucky sees that his acceptance of the food has given the human great happiness.

Lucky repeats his mission. Waits. He repeats it again. The time after that, he doesn't glance off the human's hand. He rests on it. He feels the warm hand drop slightly as he lands. The human stays mostly steady. Lucky feeds from the crumbs. He keeps his head flicking from side to side at all times. He is still alert. His heart beats quickly beneath his feathered chest. The human smiles broadly, eyes shining. Lucky blinks his thanks to the human and leaves.

Back in the Spindly Tree, Buffy is amazed. "I watched you. That was so brave!" she proclaims.

"I just felt safe," Lucky chirps. "I don't know why. The Elders say the humans are dangerous but I don't think so. They gave me food. I could feel kindness."

Lucky feels a buzz of nervous energy. He has defied the Elders. That feels wrong. And yet, the human has been friendly. That feels like a discovery.

*

Sunrise after sunrise passes. Lucky returns to the same ditch, to the same human. He recognises him easily by the thick, bristly line of hairs between his nose and mouth. Buffy joins him. Each time the human sees them, he offers more crumbs. Sometimes, he doesn't see them and together, the birds perch and watch and listen. On those occasions, they see the other nearby humans tending to the ditch or carefully trying to clean their collection of objects – especially the firing sticks. Buffy thinks that this is like a bird preening its feathers or building its nest.

Upon one visit, the human takes out a small square of paper from inside his cloth covering. It bears a lifelike image of another human. He stares fondly at the image then touches it to his puckered mouth. He clutches it against his chest before returning it safely to where it came from. Like most, this human's face is drawn and wrinkled. He looks into the distance, his eyes searching for somewhere far beyond the grey sky. He looks so full of sorrow.

Another time, they do not see the familiar human with the crumbs at first. A replacement is in his usual place. Soon, this human is tapped on the shoulder and the one they remember swaps positions with the first. More than ever, he looks weary and slouches against the side of the muddy ditch.

"The humans are unhappy," Lucky reflects after many visits. The daylight lasts longer and the darkness is shorter, now. The danger still sneaks up on them all the time.

"We see their faces filled with fear, yet they show bravery to be here in the danger," Buffy observes. The birds cast their eyes over the mud and squalor in the ditches. "I think they have loved ones elsewhere. I think they miss their homes."

"There is so little space. Are they trapped in there? Can they not leave?" asks Lucky.

"I think, perhaps, they are staying until they have completed something," the tree sparrow muses.

"Completed what?" asks Lucky.

"I'm not sure. A challenge? I don't really understand. The humans are striking the land from both sides... perhaps they feel that they must conquer it," Buffy suggests.

The pair fly farther to the west. They both passed this way when they had to flee from the grave danger, last summer. They observe another row of human ditches, then another and another. Farther than that, there are still more humans. Never does Lucky feel that the humans pose him danger. The danger comes with the bangs and screams but it is never directed towards the birds. Without exception, the humans are happy to see Lucky and Buffy visiting them.

Of course, they return to the Spindly Tree. It is their tree, where they have their branch. The kestrel is also in the Spindly Tree when they return this time. He gives a grumpy shake of his feathers. His head settles low into his body once more and he peers down at them over his large, pointed beak.

"You have not heeded my warning," he sneers.

Buffy shuffles along the branch and tilts her head to bring the kestrel into view. Lucky twitches and does not meet the kestrel's stare.

"We are careful. It is all right," Buffy says.

"I doubt that," the kestrel responds. "You have been visiting the humans. And you are still together. A chaffinch and a sparrow. Together. Hmph." He judders.

"I told you," Buffy protests. "We are friends."

"Friends? You should concentrate on surviving, not making friends."

Lucky shuffles his claws on the branch. He tucks his wing into his side. He summons the bravery that he discovered when visiting the humans.

"Um. The humans are kind," he mumbles. "They

choose to give us crumbs."

"Ha! You are foolish but at least you picked a side," the kestrel affirms. With that, he unfurls his mighty wings. A lingering glare follows. Then, he launches away, leaving the Spindly Tree quivering in his wake.

Lucky looks forlornly at Buffy. "Did we pick a side? I didn't mean to choose a side," he says.

"Well, we *have* spent all our time on one side. We didn't *pick* a side, though, did we?"

"We should visit the other side of the Land of No Man's. See the other humans," suggests Lucky.

"How could they be any different from the ones we have seen?" Buffy asks. "Both sides fire upon the land. Both bring danger."

Lucky thinks. He shuffles his claws again. He twitches his head. "We have to find out. We can't choose a side without even meaning to. Maybe it will help us understand," he chitters.

Minds made up, the birds fly to the east side

of the Land of No Man's. The distance is not at all far. The opposite sides of human ditches are separated by no more than a furlong: the width of a large field. Farther along, in places, the gap is even less. And yet, the humans from each side never meet.

Lucky and Buffy glide over the eastern ditches. These almost mirror those on the west side, remarkable in similarity. Long, deep, complex valleys line the land. The same smooth pieces of wood prop up the ditch sides, fashioned into wide, flat panels. There are sandbags, scattered objects and hundreds and hundreds of humans. All look the same. To Lucky, they look no more, and no less, dangerous. They have hard head coverings. They have matching earth-coloured cloth body coverings. They, too, brandish firing sticks strapped across their bodies.

"I don't think they look any happier," chirrups Buffy. Her eyes dart across humans who are eating from metal containers or sleeping restlessly or moving purposefully through their ditches.

"They are busying themselves but they seem to

be waiting, just like the others," Lucky observes.

"Waiting for what?" Buffy chirps.

"Perhaps for the darkness," Lucky suggests, "when they must bring their attack to the land."

"Why, though?" asks Buffy. "What threat is this place?"

As the birds hover in the air, the humans shuffle in the ground. In the ditches farthest from the Land of No Man's, there is more eating, resting or other duties being performed. In the ditches closest, the humans are alert, like the birds. They keep watch.

Here, a human spots the birds. It is just like on the other side. This time, Lucky feels more prepared. Worry still perches in the back of his mind but his experience brings him more courage. He tilts and bobs his head. The human smiles. This human taps the limb of another next to him, then points. The second human takes out leaves of paper from his pouch. He frantically makes marks on them, looking straight at Lucky, then back at his paper, many times.

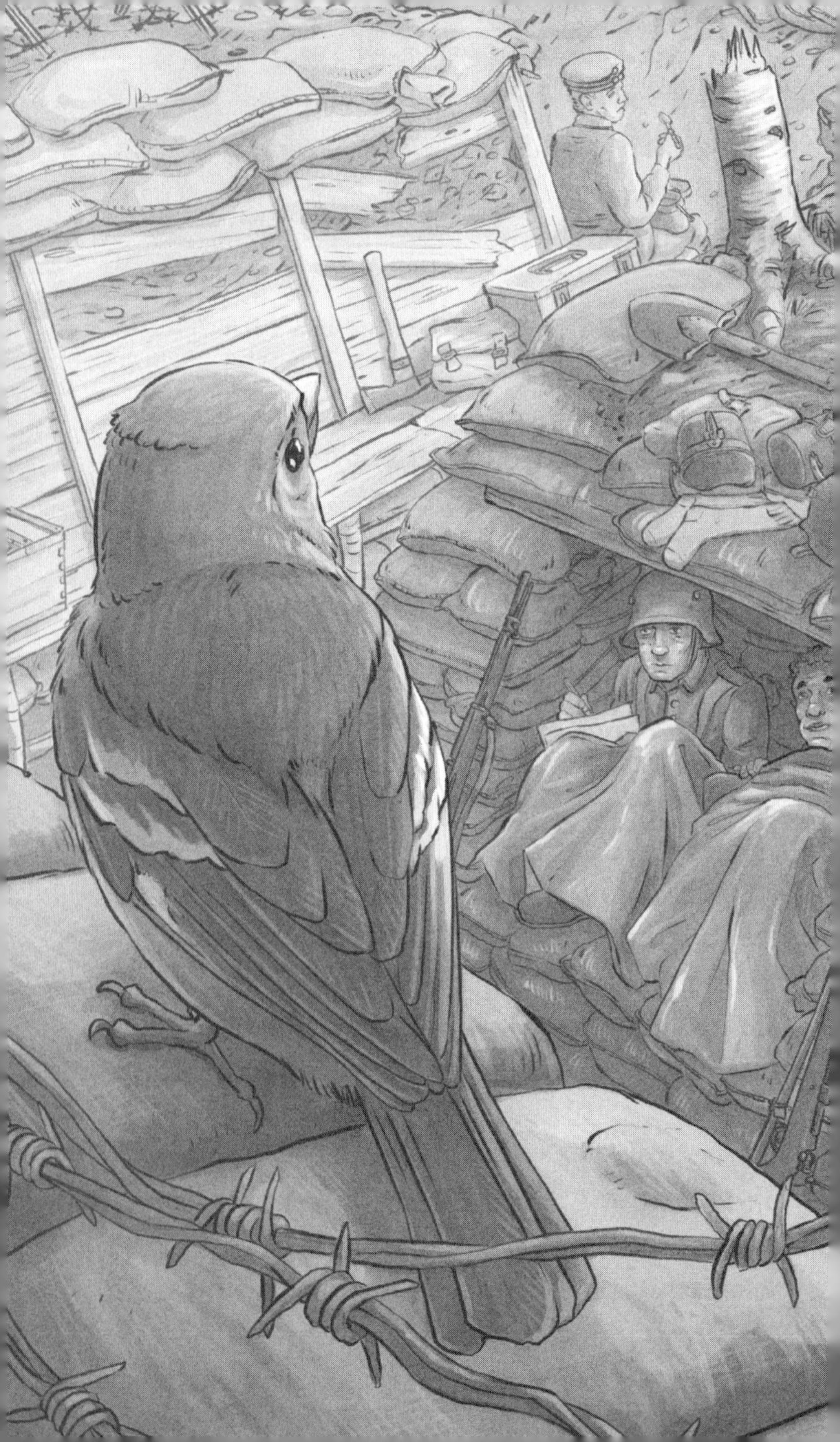

Eventually, the second human shows his paper to the first. They both smile. Satisfied, Lucky swoops. Over the humans' heads, he loops and glances down.

He is astonished.

The human has created a picture of him. Lucky is depicted on the paper, just as he had perched a moment ago. His heart flutters as fast as his wings.

The two birds settle in the Spindly Tree.

"Did you see what they did?" Lucky asks. "It was a picture of me."

"Yes!" tweets Buffy. "It was beautiful."

*

The pair spend many more sunrises frequenting the human ditches, not just on one side but on both. In the morning, Lucky feeds from crumbs offered by the human with the line of bristly hairs. In the afternoon, he sits and another human makes pictures of him. Buffy feeds and

45

poses, too. They fly in circles, performing. Every time, they draw smiles from the humans. Yet, when the humans do not notice them, their muddy faces look filled with sadness.

The more the birds visit, the more they listen. The ditches of humans on each side have much in common. They all seem brave and determined, yet perhaps this is a mask for their fear. Often, they look at their pictures: the loved ones whom they must miss. Lucky so dearly wants to help them.

After their visits, the birds always return to the Spindly Tree.

"I don't think the humans live here," Lucky says from his side of the branch. "I think their home is still somewhere else."

"I think you are right," Buffy agrees. "They look at pictures of other humans who are not here. They look lovingly, sadly. I think they make messages to send on paper, too."

"Yes. Sometimes, they are receiving messages on their papers! That's when they look most joyful.

Most other times, their faces carry only misery."

"Even when they try to sleep, they wriggle and writhe. They are never relaxed here."

"Like us! So why have they been here for so long?" Lucky wonders aloud.

"Maybe they must conquer the land first," Buffy muses.

*

The two birds give great thought to what they should do. Eventually, a plan forms.

"The humans are on both sides. They are always happy to see us, right?" Lucky asks.

"Sure," Buffy agrees.

"Apart from that, they look troubled, cheerless. They want to succeed. They want to go home to see their loved ones."

"Yes," says Buffy. "What is your point?"

"I know how we can help!" he announces, almost breathless.

"Go on." She is intrigued.

"We must rally the other birds. Visit the humans, without being scared. Sing to them, accept their crumbs, let them make pictures of us, fly above them to bring them smiles. Show them kindness."

"How will this help?"

"They are so downhearted. If we raise their spirits, it might help them to succeed – help them to reach the end. We can bring glee to their hearts. Then, they may be able to go home. Peace will return to the Land of No Man's and everywhere nearby."

"Are you sure?" asks Buffy, doubtfully.

"No," admits Lucky, "but it's worth a try. Come on! Let's ask the Elders!"

*

The two birds wait for two sunsets before returning to visit the Elders when they know the wise birds will be congregating. They land at the base of the three branchless trunks. There is no sign of the blackbirds but the yellowhammer spies them immediately.

"What is your business, young ones?" he asks.

"We think we know how to help the humans," Lucky responds nervously.

"Help them?" chimes the cuckoo. "Help them to do what? They have brought danger to the fields. They have torn up the earth with their machines. Their noise and smoke ruin our skies."

"But that's just it," Buffy attempts. "If we work together with them, we can help them to achieve their goals and they will leave. We think they want to go back to their own homes. We think they have loved ones, whom they miss."

The nightingale, wise and watchful as ever, nods. She tilts her head and waits for a sign from the yellowhammer. The yellowhammer twitches his tail and blinks. A signal is passed between them.

"What are you suggesting?" the yellowhammer asks. Lucky looks at Buffy. He wants to speak up, to be braver.

"We want to bring joy and kindness to the humans. We think that they are kind, too. If we raise their spirits, we can help them. If we all sing, we can rally them, together."

Again, the yellowhammer and the nightingale exchange glances. It is the cuckoo who chirps first.

"It is a beautiful plan. We should let them try."

"Very well," the nightingale agrees. "You are granted permission. You will need to visit the flocks yourselves. It is up to each of them to join you, if they wish to."

Delighted, the pair set off again immediately, visiting each flock one by one. Lucky asks the larks if they will sing in the early mornings. Buffy rounds up the nightingales to sing in the evenings. All the flocks agree. Robins, thrushes, blackbirds all join the chorus.

Birdsong is soon filling the air more than ever before. Sunrise after sunset after sunrise, swallows dart and dive through the air over the heads of the humans. Hedge sparrows land on the shrubs around the ditches.

All of the birds are less fearful of the humans, now. Lucky and Buffy have spread the word that the humans are no danger to them. When the danger strikes, the birds take cover. When it is done, they sing again. The joy of the skies contrasts with the gloom below. The beauty of the birdsong counters the blasts of the firing machines.

Even more birds arrive who have never been seen in the Land of No Man's before. The baby robin of two summers ago is no longer a baby, no longer so cautious. He sits on one of the firing sticks belonging to a human. Most agree that the birds and the humans have grown closer. The humans gaze in awe at the birds. The birds revel in bringing smiles to the humans' faces.

Sitting in the Spindly Tree, Lucky and Buffy are joined by a willow warbler. She is unfamiliar. For a moment, she makes no sound. Then arrives

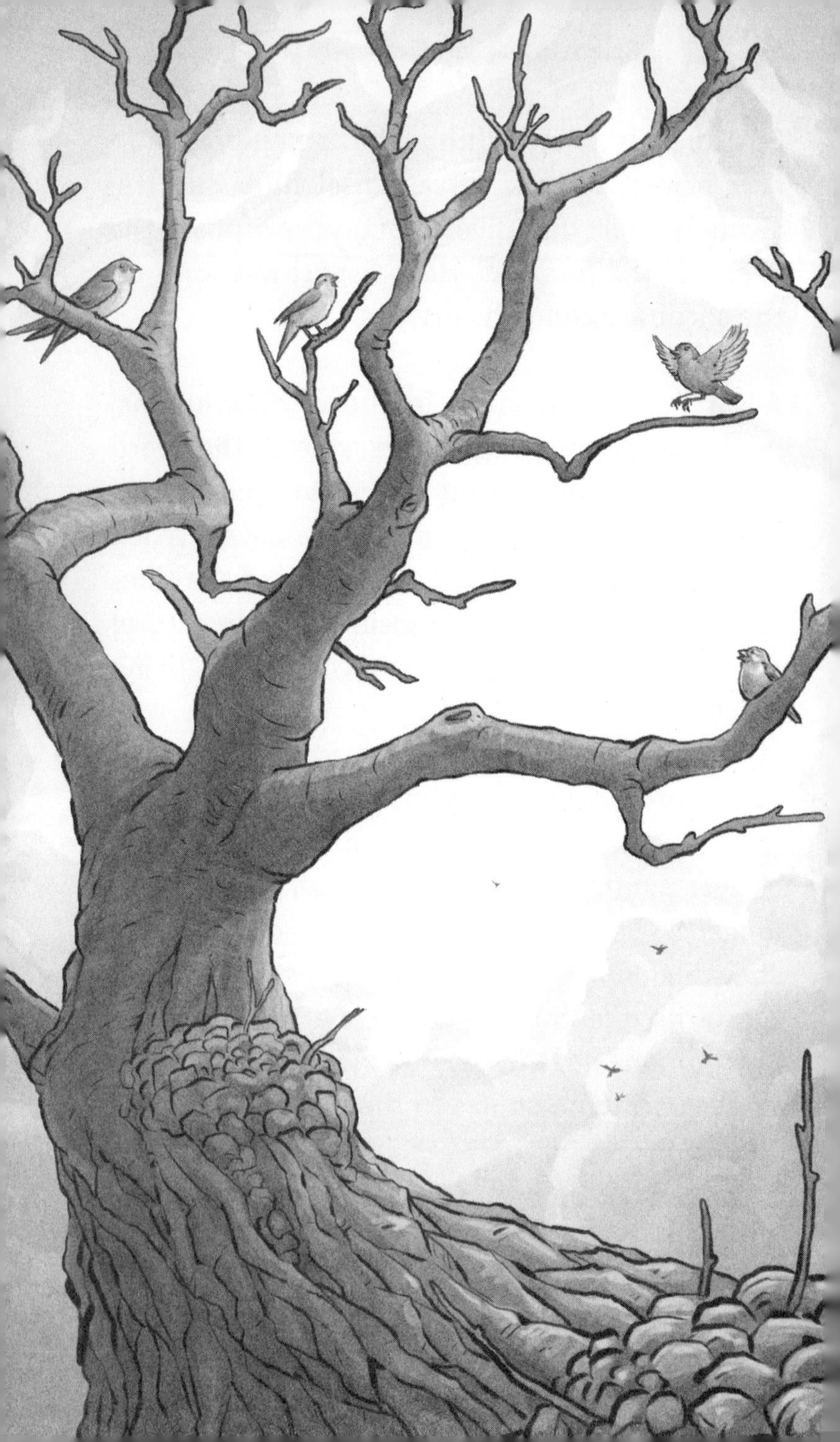

a sand martin. He perches next to the warbler. Lucky and Buffy twitch and exchange glances.

"Um. Hello," Lucky chirrups curiously. It is more of a question than a greeting.

"Hey," the warbler chirps back. "Are you the finch and the sparrow?"

Buffy answers. "That might be us. Why?"

"We have come from fields afar. We have heard about the gathering for peace."

Lucky hops on his branch and twists. He feels a buzz of excitement.

"You've heard and come to join us? Here, where there is danger?" he chitters.

"We heard that the humans were not a danger to us," the sand martin chips in. "We heard that there is more food than anywhere, here: insects on the ground, crumbs from the humans. We heard that you were singing for peace."

"Yes!" Lucky dances on his branch. He cannot

believe the message is spreading so far and wide. "Yes, that's right! Will you stay and sing?"

"Of course," replies the warbler. "We are here with our flocks. We wanted to find you. We heard that it all started with the friendship of the finch and the sparrow. We wanted to say thank you!"

Lucky chirps a tweet of happiness.

"We are friends, too," says the martin, "even though we are from different flocks."

"Just like us!" exclaims Lucky.

"Just like you," agrees the warbler.

Together, the four birds fly from the tree. They swoop through the Land of No Man's. Giving a guided tour, Lucky notices how many more birds there are. Below, the land is still desolate, caked with mud and despair. In the skies and all around, the birds sing. They fly from one landing spot to another. The robins and the blackbirds, the swallows and the swifts; the warblers and the sand martins; the chaffinch who has almost forgotten his wonky wing and the tree sparrow who hears very well on one side, just not the other.

Beyond the Land of No Man's, there are more little wooden crosses than ever. There is hope emerging, too: new, bright red poppy flowers are appearing. Their sprinkles of colour are creeping ever closer towards the brown, trampled earth around which they are scattered. There are other colours dotted not far away: green leaves, yellow dandelions and blue cornflowers.

*

The hope carries the birds – and the humans – through to autumn. However, that means time for the Big Journey again. This time, Lucky will make the Big Journey without Ma or Pa. He is no longer a juvenile. He will go alone. Next year, he might have his own young family to look after, too.

As the time comes to embark, Lucky hopes that he will leave the dangers behind for the last time. He hopes to return to find peace; that together, the birds have brought enough glee to the humans' hearts for them all to win.

The Final Summer

1918

Lucky's hopes crumble. Another winter has been spent away. Yet his return brings no change in the Land of No Man's. It is clear that the fields have taken even more damage during his time away.

This year, he must help to find a nesting place for a mating partner. Buffy is back, too, and also seeking a nesting place of her own. The Spindly Tree casts a ghoulish shadow along the ground. The boggy earth is layered with more debris, more remains, more misery. The land is rotting.

In their ditches, the humans are woozy with fatigue. Some lie without moving. The pair seek out the human with the line of bristly hairs on his face who always gave them crumbs. Sadly, there is no sign of him, nor the others who seemed to be his friends.

Different humans are in their place now – different, but in equal distress.

The fear on some faces is more stark than ever. Wide eyes of fresh-faced humans, looking even younger than those they have replaced, search the skies with expectant horror.

The human who makes the pictures looks relieved to see the birds return. He tries immediately to create a new picture when he spots Lucky but, in the months since they saw him, his hands have started to shake. He makes a few unsteady attempts to mark the paper. Then, with a sigh, he gives up. The birds can feel his low spirits. They fly away, leaving him clutching his face in his trembling hands.

"It hasn't worked," says Buffy. Her head droops in despair. "Everything is still the same as when we left."

"Maybe it can still change," Lucky tries to argue. "Now that we are all returning, we can try again. We can sing and fly. The humans look like they need cheer more than ever."

Before Buffy can reply, another shadow is cast. From overhead swoops the kestrel. He lands on something which protrudes from the ground. It is a human's hard, leather foot covering. The kestrel shakes out his wings then folds them neatly into his body, adjusting the grip of his claws on the object. His bandit eyes and sharp, pointed beak stay trained on Lucky.

"Do you two never learn? Do you still talk of singing and peace?"

Lucky summons his courage in reply. "Yes." He puffs out his feathery chest. The kestrel is four times his size. "The humans are kind. We can help them."

"You have not seen what I have seen while you have all been away on your journeys. Your humans have caged birds behind those ditches," the kestrel says solemnly.

"No, it's not true," chirps Buffy, appalled.

"Go and see for yourselves. Fly to the farthest ditches. Find the wheeled boxes. You'll see our kind imprisoned – canaries singing behind bars.

The humans are not your friends."

Lucky and Buffy exchange glances and twitches. For the first time since last summer, Lucky feels the familiar ache of his wing again.

"Want to know more?" the kestrel continues. "Find the pigeons. Humans have them trapped in baskets. They send them into danger to carry their messages. The humans do not care for us."

"They do. They are kind," insists Lucky. "We choose to help them. If the humans win, we can all have peace again."

"Hmph. Kind? Peace? You still don't see it. They are hurting each other! All this danger – they send it themselves from their ditches to those on the other side. They even leave their ditches to attack their kin. You will get hurt, too, if you continue."

Overhead, a pigeon flies. The kestrel's predatory eyes are drawn to it. Powerfully, he propels himself into the air. With long, threatening beats of his wings, he is gone, up towards the clouds.

"Are they really sending danger to each other? Do they attack one another?" Lucky asks. His head twitches in confusion. He has never considered this before. There were the stories of humans leaving their ditches to cause harm. He had not seen it and had dismissed the rumours. The ache in his wing intensifies, progressively gnawing at him inside.

"Perhaps it is so," Buffy admits, her head drooping dolefully. "They show such kindness to us. I don't understand – how can they be so unkind to one another? They are all the same."

Lucky has no answer.

As the summer weeks pass, the kestrel's rumours filter through the flocks. The next dawn chorus is stunted, enthusiasm curbed; the one after that is even quieter. The birds who have returned from their Big Journeys share Lucky's disappointment. Those who stayed behind had already lost their hope, long ago.

The sunsets bring more danger than ever. Crackles and explosions light up the darkness. Roaring, pounding, blasting sounds fill the air.

Occasionally, there are shouts and screams from the humans. Lucky wishes that he couldn't hear the anguish.

His eyesight is still sharp. Even in the darkest darkness, he sees a scene that he wishes he did not witness. Amid the noise and chaos, a barrage of humans leave their ditch on one side. They charge, violently. Not content with sending danger through the skies, they take their attack on foot across the Land of No Man's. The rumours become undeniable: bloodshed and brutality is unleashed across the usually empty expanse of mud.

Lucky struggles for the right words or the right actions. During daylight, he hops and skitters from place to place. Trying to avoid the horrors revealed by each sunrise, he continues to look for a nesting site.

Everywhere, he just finds worry or danger. During darkness, he hunkers into shrubbery, hiding among the highest branches. These dangers have lasted more than three summers. When, he wonders, will it end? Why does it happen?

At the Spindly Tree, which he has also avoided, he finds Buffy in the daylight. They have not seen each other for several sunrises. She is building a nest.

"Here?" Lucky chirrups in shock. "Are you building your nest here?"

She drops a small twig from her beak. "There is nowhere else any safer between the ditches. We know this tree so well. It feels like home."

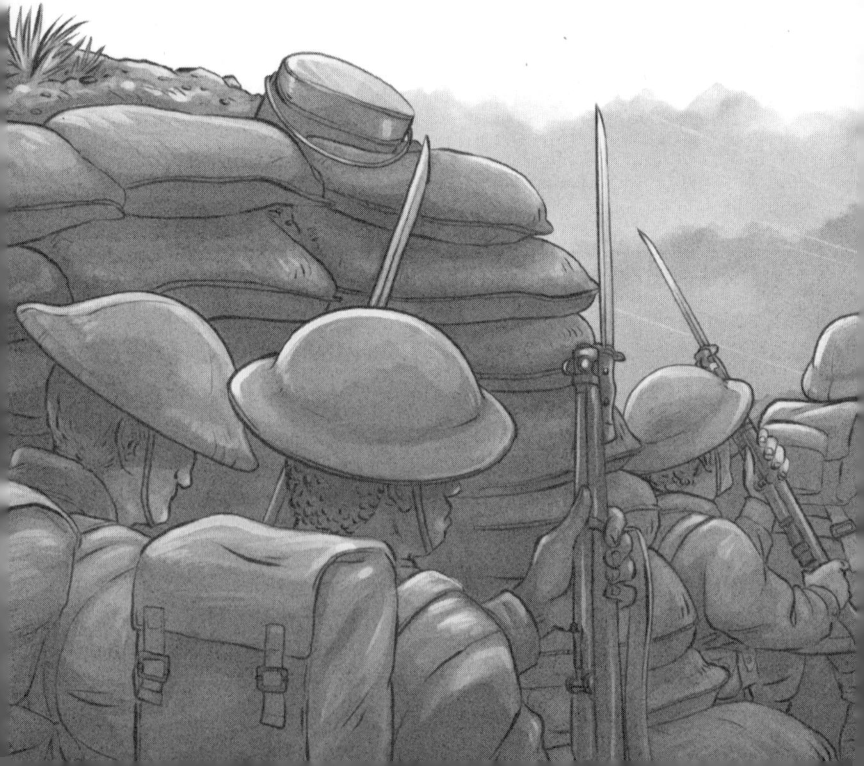

Word is spreading through the Land of No Man's. There have been birds lost or injured. Others have heard or seen the humans charging through darkness across the mud.

"Have you heard?" Buffy asks him. "A skylark was injured. Her wing was caught by some flying metal. They say she was taken by the humans."

Lucky gulps, as though a huge worm were caught in his throat.

"What have we done? Have we invited birds here into danger? Have we misjudged the humans? Can this be our fault?" Lucky's questions spill from his beak.

"We have not caused it," she says. "We have only tried our best. We did not bring the danger."

"But what can we do now?" Lucky asks, his head twitching from side to side as he chirps. The danger feels almost always present, now, even when it is quiet.

"I must finish building. Then, maybe we should visit the Elders again," suggests Buffy.

Lucky nods.

*

Buffy spends the rest of the summer building a home and caring for her chicks. Then, once more, she and Lucky visit the site of the three branchless trunks at dusk. The blackbirds are present again, along with a skylark whom they have not seen before. There is no sign of the cuckoo, this time.

The nightingale confirms the kestrel's revelations. "It is true. We have seen the caged canaries. Pigeons have also flown through but they have been spotted later in baskets." She turns to Buffy and her caring eyes flutter. "You need to be more careful, now. You must concentrate on your own young."

The yellowhammer chirps harshly at Lucky. "Need we remind you? You will soon be an Elder yourself. You must show responsibility, now."

The skylark speaks up about the missing bird from her flock. "The missing skylark is Ruffles. She was in flight one morning, just a couple of sunrises ago. Another lark reported seeing an explosion. Everyone scattered into the sky. Debris was thrown in all directions. A tiny piece struck Ruffles on her side. She cried out and spiralled to the ground, near the human ditches.

"She hopped along the ground, searching for shelter. There is a rumour that a human climbed from the ditch to capture her. She has not been seen since."

"So, what now? What should we do?" asks Lucky.

"It is for you to decide," says one of the blackbirds, looking more weary than before.

This visit to the Elders leaves both Lucky and Buffy downhearted and unsure. They fly their separate ways.

*

As autumn washes over the Land of No Man's, one event shatters Lucky's last resolve.

Rain tumbles from the skies above. Bitter wind blows through the trees. A flurry of danger comes with the rumbling clouds. Bangs, thuds, booms. Thick smoke fills the moist air; pockets of smouldering debris litter the Land of No Man's. Birds scatter to foliage farther afield.

First, they hunker away from the stormy sky, then they cower at the threats added by the humans.

Worst of all, stories are shared that a nesting tree has been blown clean out of the ground – not by the strength of wind and rain but by a human blast.

It reminds Lucky of his first nest as a chick – his nest that was blown out of the ground and his wing, which aches as a constant reminder. Yet the news is even worse. This time, the displaced tree is the Spindly Tree. The stricken nest is Buffy's nest. Inside were Buffy's newly hatched chicks.

Some birds take flight. They say that they are leaving forever. The Land of No Man's cannot be trusted any longer. Other birds pledge to sing no more. When news reaches Lucky, he flies immediately back to the Spindly Tree.

The danger is gone from the air, for now – but it has left devastation behind.

The tree is dislodged from the ground. It points to the stormy sky at an odd angle, no longer straight up. At its base, a knotted ball of roots is thick with mud, protruding above the ground.

Lucky flaps around in the drizzle, unsure where it is safe to land. Incredibly, the nest is still wedged into a nook of branches. It is still in the tree but the tree is not quite in the ground. Buffy is perched precariously on the edge of the

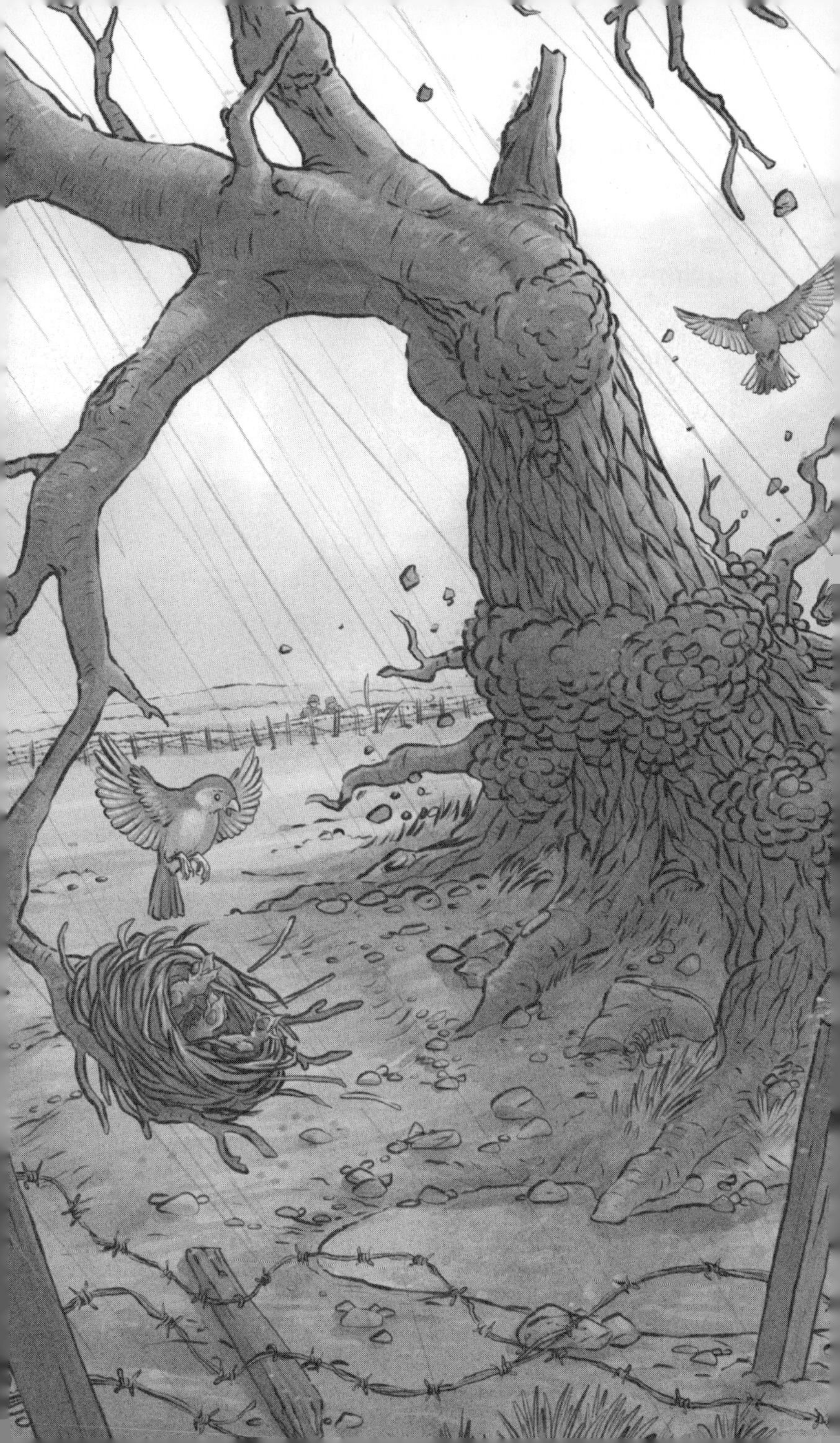

nest. She squeaks and squeals with panic and confusion.

Lucky swoops closer. He daren't land on the tree for fear of his tiny weight toppling it over. He sees that the chicks are all alive, trembling and sodden. Miraculously, they have survived but they are not safe yet.

A human rises from the eastern ditch. It is the friend of the human who makes the pictures. He is followed by several more; they rise together out of the safety of their deep, waterlogged hole.

Lucky flutters in the air above the Spindly Tree.

The humans do something remarkable – something Lucky has never seen. In the pouring rain, they hold on to their head covers and launch themselves out of their ditch. Running like rabbits would run from a fox, they hurtle towards the tree. A trail of thick sludge splashes up behind them from the pounding of their squelching steps. Their firing sticks swing wildly about their bodies. They are not using them.

Slipping and sliding, they reach the tree.

Between them, they grab hold of the trunk and, with a mix of strength and care, they wrestle the roots back into the now rain-filled hole from which they were torn.

The Spindly Tree stands upright and tall again, replanted. Frantically, the humans kick the swampy earth over the roots. They make a mound over the roots, then stamp it down, holding the tree steady.

Just as quickly as they came, they turn and hurtle away. Sloppy mud sprays in their wake. Lucky watches them reach their ditch. He sees them jump feet first into it, caught by more cheering humans as they land. The whole episode is a mud-splattered blur.

Lucky flutters down onto the tree, the tall-again, upright Spindly Tree. Buffy's squeaks and squeals have turned to chirps of relief. Her joy is unbridled. Lucky cannot believe what he has seen.

"They saved us," Buffy chirrups, dripping wet. "How can it be true that they are cruel?"

"They are not. This is proof. We must not be

sorrowful that the danger happens," Lucky proclaims. "We must spread the word that kindness can still win. When we sing for them, the humans show such kindness to us. I know that they can show kindness to one another if we keep trying."

"No one will listen, now. Flocks have started to leave. What about the stories of the pigeons, the canaries, the skylark who is still missing?"

"It is time not to listen to stories but to find facts," Lucky declares. "I will stay with you here until the next sunrise. You must look after the chicks. Then, I will investigate."

*

As promised, each of the following sunrises, Lucky investigates. He brings back daily news to Buffy as the darkness begins to last much longer and the air turns colder.

He discovers that the pigeons are using their skills to help. Humans send them with messages. They live in lofts made for them by humans and are given food, and they fly happily back to their coops. They are loved. A pigeon declares that the greatest danger he has faced was not from humans. It was from a kestrel who tried to chase him from the sky. Buffy is horrified at this news.

Nearby, the canaries are indeed in cages, Lucky discovers, but they sing merrily. They, too, are loved by the humans. The kindness is shared. Humans feed the canaries, give them water, talk to them. The canaries sing to comfort the injured humans and bring them cheer. They exist together happily.

Lucky even finds Ruffles, the missing skylark. She has been taken by the humans, it is true. For several sunrises, the humans have been saving their crumbs for the injured lark, nursing her. It reminds Lucky of the human who used to feed him crumbs. They haven't seen him this summer. With nourishment, Ruffles' wing is healing. Then, she will return to her flock. The humans have helped her, not captured her.

Each piece of news gives Buffy more hope. Lucky's feathers tingle with excitement as he relays it. His mind is made up about what to do. He flies from flock to flock, rallying the other remaining birds. He tells the story of the nest in the Spindly Tree being saved. Once more, he visits the blackbirds, the robins, the nightingales. He finds the warbler and the sand martin who came to the Land of No Man's to sing for peace. They have remained there. They have remained together.

"Let's be positive," he tells them all each time. "Let's sing again! We need everyone for one more effort. We can still bring glee. We can bring change. One last push. This time, let's fill the humans with so much joy that their kindness extends to each other, too."

One by one, the flocks join in again. The nightingales sing at sunset. The skylarks sing before dawn. All the birds join in with a longer, louder chorus, every single sunrise. The weary humans are woken each day by birdsong. In return, they offer smiles and crumbs as thanks. Each new day still brings danger but, regardless, the birds sing on.

The chorus continues sunrise after sunrise until, one day, a change occurs.

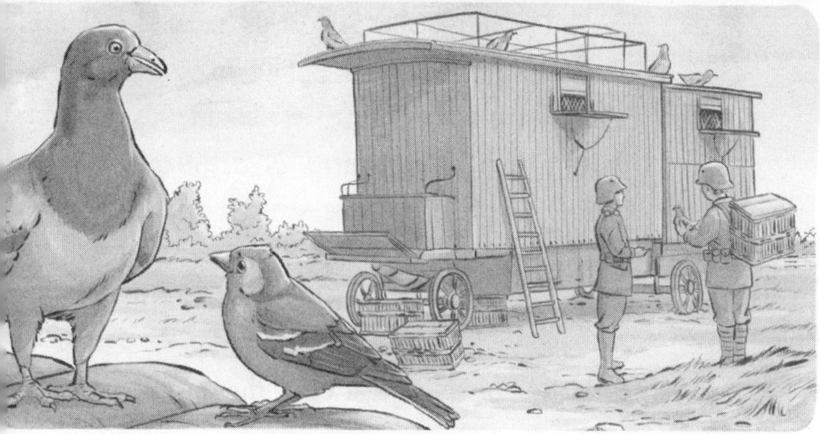

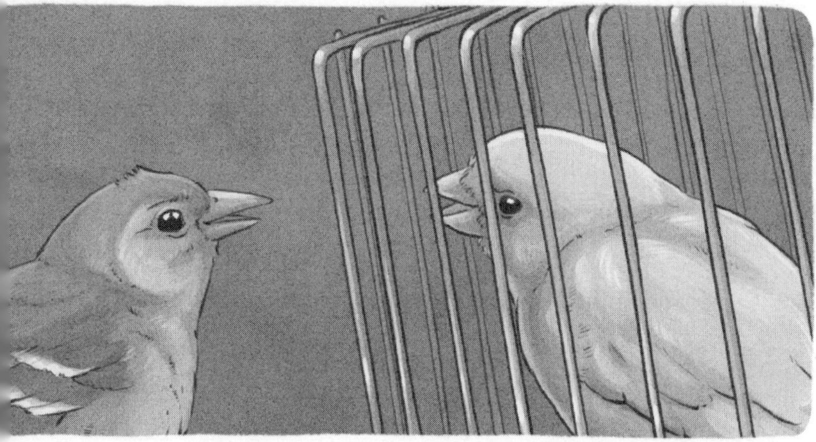

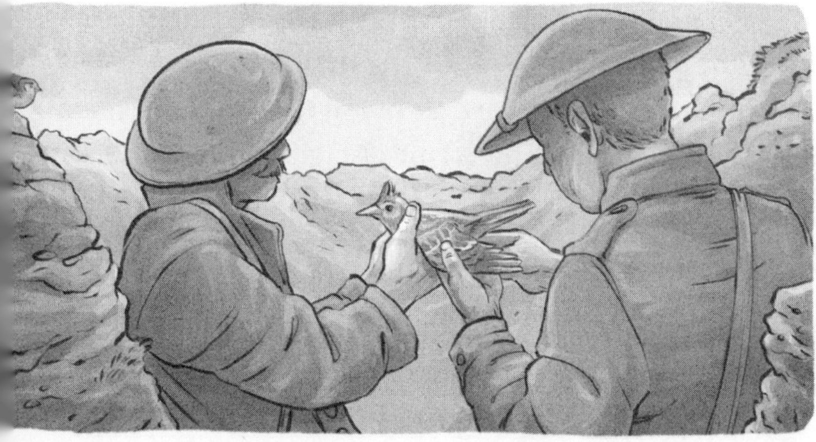

Lucky flies through the Land of No Man's and senses the change. Something is different. No danger comes. There are more smiles on human faces, cheers even. They look less tense, less fraught. There is something different in the air.

At first, the other birds refuse to believe it. Yet, no more danger or noise occurs. None this daylight, nor any the next. A ripple runs through the Land of No Man's: the dangers are over. It is a ripple of relief.

The humans begin to retreat. The closest ditches become empty, unoccupied. Only discarded objects and remains lie, left behind.

As the eastern ditches empty, one human catches Lucky's attention. It is the one who has made pictures of him. The human waves a leaf of paper at Lucky, wipes at his eyes, then turns away. Lucky hovers in the air and watches the human growing farther away through the maze of ditches until he is out of sight.

"They are leaving," he tells Buffy. The pair perch, of course, in the Spindly Tree. Lucky clutches onto a branch. Buffy sits in her empty nest. Her nestlings have fledged. They have survived. The tree still stands, after all this time.

"It can't be," Buffy replies. "After so long. It's hard to believe."

"We did it," blinks Lucky.

The strangest sound of all begins to envelop the dusk over the Land of No Man's. It is the sound of peace.

After the War

1919

A tree stands in a field formerly known as the Land of No Man's. It is a spindly tree but its branches sprout tiny, green leaves.

Below the tree, the once barren soil is alive with colour. The land is beginning to be revitalised. Tall, green stems reach up out of the earth and sway in the breeze, topped with bright red poppy flowers. In the fields beyond, there are more colours – greens and yellows and blues – mingling with the red.

It is by no means a complete transformation; the scars remain. Deep ditches, banked-up earth and wooden stumps serve as reminders of previous summers. Pushing out of the ground are more little wooden crosses than ever.

On a branch of the tree sit two birds. One is a chaffinch and one is a tree sparrow. They are Elders. One has a frail wing; one has poor hearing. They chirp contentedly about the stories they recall and the experiences they have shared in that tree. They never did pick a side.

The pair tell stories of their friendship and adventures to their offspring, who they hope will never have to live through the same experiences. The future is safe now for generations of birds but when even they are gone, the land and the poppies will still remember what happened here.

The birds' merry chirping and tweeting carries easily across the carpet of red flowers. Birdsong and breeze: the sound of peace still reigns.

Afterword

The First World War lasted from 28th July 1914 to 11th November 1918. This story is just a story, but the human soldiers and the birds of Flanders Fields are real.

Birds did live and nest around No Man's Land during the height of the war. Because of the decay and churned-up earth, there were many insects for them to eat. There are real reports of nests in field guns and in used shell casings, and an injured bird was nursed back to health with crumbs by soldiers in their trench. A robin was said to perch regularly on a soldier's bayonet. Birds did not really have any influence on how or why the war came to an end. The presence of the birds did, however, raise the spirits of soldiers during difficult times.

Canaries were kept in cages to sing and cheer up injured troops; they were also used by the soldiers to test for toxic gases. Soldiers used carrier pigeons for a variety of messaging purposes, including to send updates back from behind enemy lines. Pigeons were even honoured with awards for their services during the war and credited with saving the lives of stranded soldiers by ensuring their messages were delivered.

In 1916, a British newspaper reported that a tree with a nest in it was uprooted by shellfire near a trench. The soldiers replanted it in a shell hole and found the trembling but uninjured bird still in its nest.

It is not known how many wild birds were affected by the war. However, it is estimated that eight and a half million troops were killed in battle. A further twenty-one million were wounded. An estimated thirteen million civilians were also killed.

Poppies grew over the battlefields after the end of the war and have now become a symbol of remembrance for all those who have died in conflict.

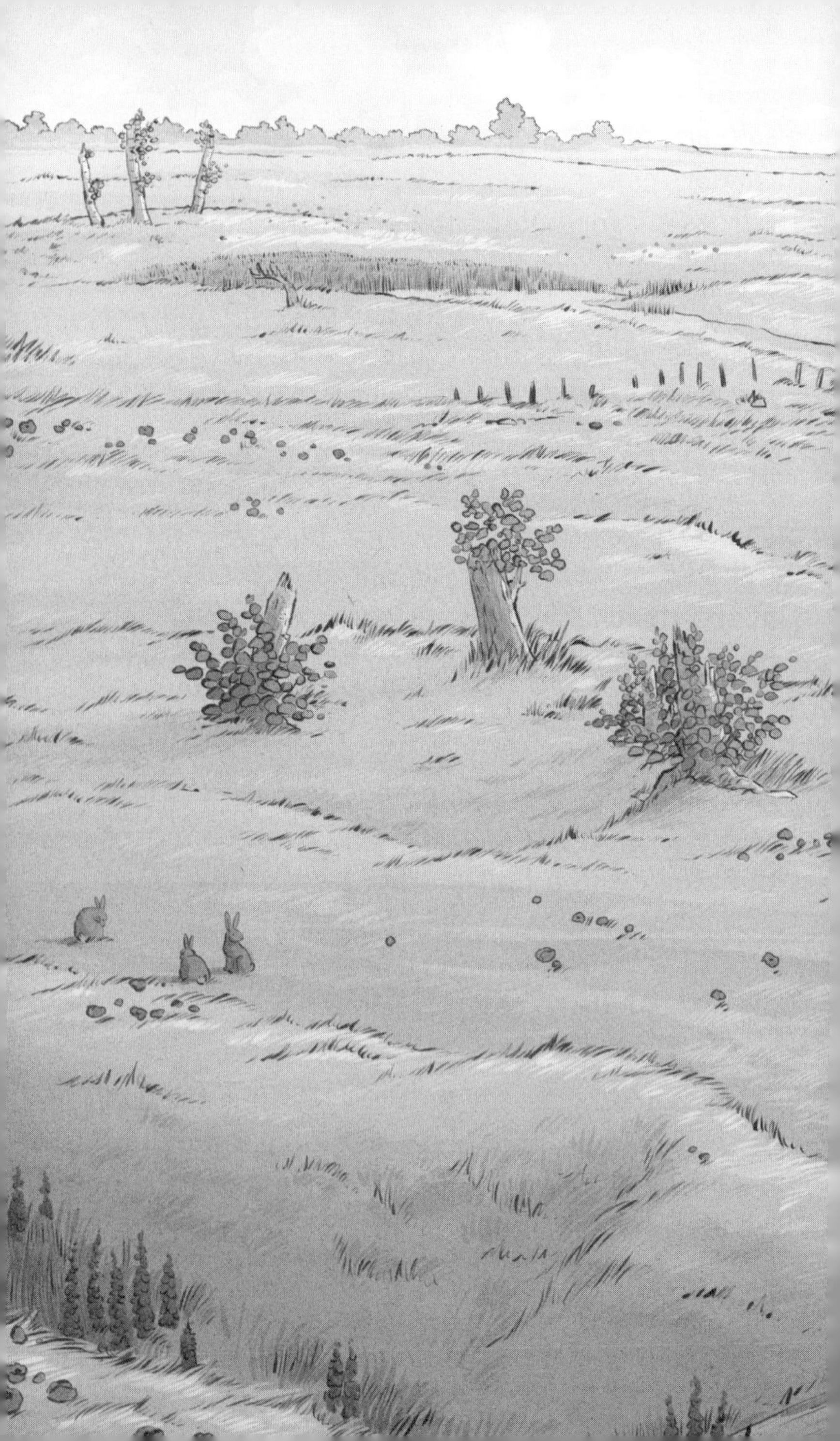

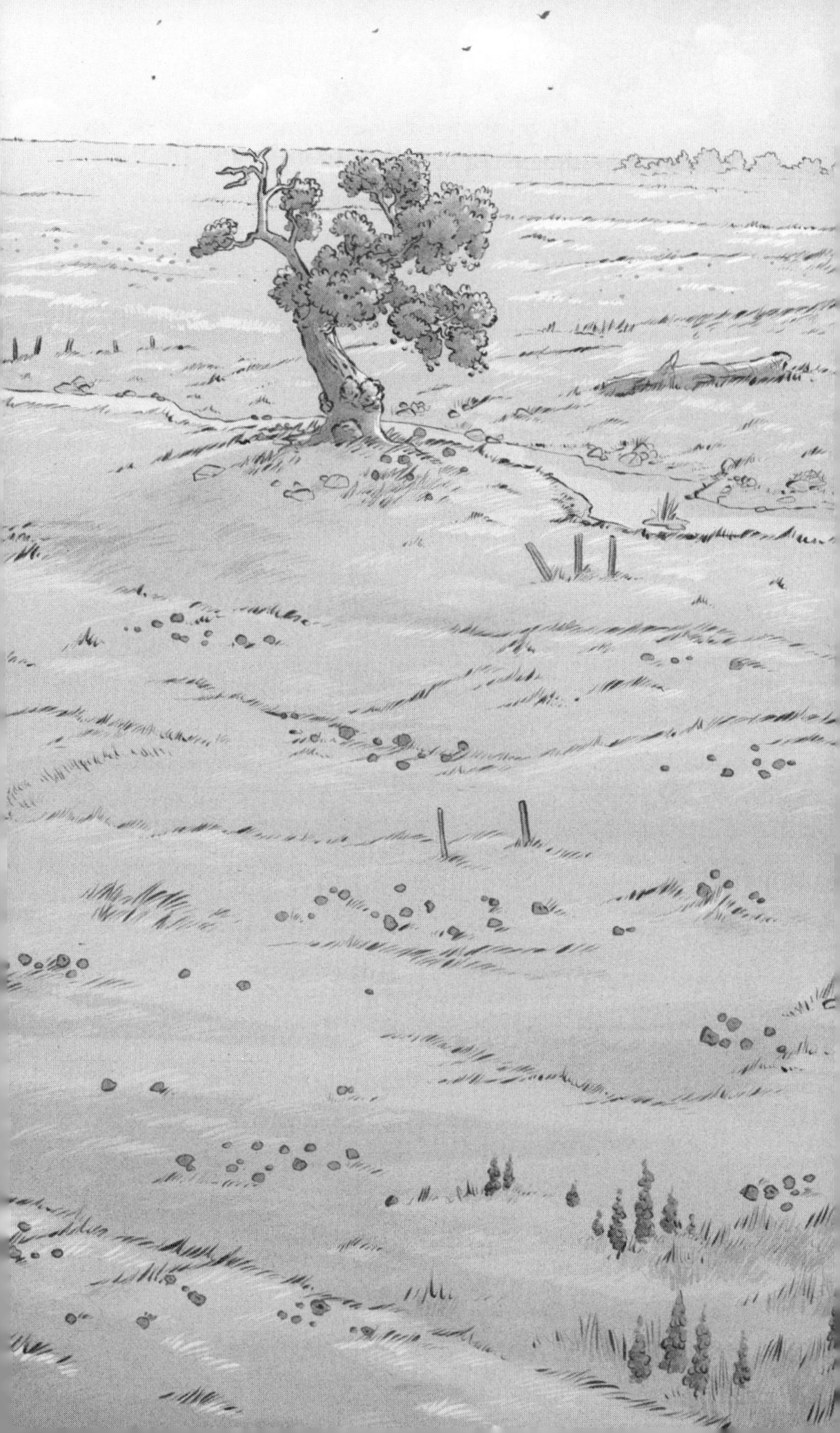

How much can you remember about the story? Take this quiz to find out!

1 How did Lucky Half-Wing get his name?

2 Who are the Elders?

3 What species of bird is Buffy?

4 What does the soldier offer to Lucky in his hand?

Answers: 1. his nest was blown out of the tree and his wing was damaged 2. a group of birds who meet every fourth sunset 3. a tree sparrow 4. crumbs

Challenge

There are many different species of bird in this story. Can you find six species of bird hidden in this word search?

K	Y	C	K	S	P	P
E	R	O	U	K	L	X
S	A	P	U	C	R	P
T	N	W	Y	R	K	A
R	A	X	O	L	U	O
E	C	B	L	N	W	O
L	I	N	V	I	B	U
N	W	O	R	R	A	P

Discussion Time

? What is your impression of 'the Land of No Man's' setting?

? *'You should pick a side and stay there.'* Do you agree with what the kestrel says to Lucky and Buffy? Why or why not?

? How does Lucky's character change throughout the story?

? What do you think the purpose of the Afterword is?

Discover more from Twinkl Originals...
Continue the learning! Explore the library of The Birds of Flanders Fields activities, games and classroom resources at twinkl.com/originals.

Welcome to the world of Twinkl Originals!

Board books for ages 0-3

Picture books for ages 3-7

Longer stories for ages 7-11

Books delivered to your door

Enjoy original works of fiction in beautiful printed form, delivered to you each half term and yours to keep!

1 Join the club at twinkl.com/book-club

2 Sign up to our Ultimate membership.

3 Make your selection – we'll take care of the rest!

The Twinkl Originals app

Now, you can read Twinkl Originals stories on the move! Enjoy a broad library of Twinkl Originals eBooks, fully accessible offline.

Search 'Twinkl Originals' in the App Store or on Google Play.

LOOK OUT FOR THE NEXT BOOK CLUB DELIVERY

When Daisy's school gives her the opportunity to view a charity's rainforest webcam feed in South America, she knows that it's a once-in-a-lifetime experience. What she doesn't expect is an unlikely video-caller with a very serious problem! Follow Pedro the potoo as he explores each layer of the Amazon rainforest. Will Daisy answer the animals' cry for help?

COMING DECEMBER 2021

Can't wait? Get the digital version at twinkl.com/originals